Giant lobsters freed

From a newspaper article in *The New York Times*

Any [lobster] old enough to weigh 25 pounds is entitled to [remain] in the deep blue sea. That's how the State of Maine sees it.

Shirley, the 25-pounder, and Bob, who weighs nearly 20 pounds, have been in the Maine waters for a long time. Maine law protects [them]. Unfortunately, Shirley and Bob were snagged in a dragger's net and brought to Rhode Island. . . .

D0888186

For my mother, Sylvia Margolin

PUFFIN BOOKS
Published by the Penguin Group
Penguin Putnam Inc., 375 Hudson Street, New York, New York 10014, U.S.A.
Penguin Books Ltd, 27 Wrights Lane, London W8 5TZ, England
Penguin Books Australia Ltd, Ringwood, Victoria, Australia
Penguin Books Canada Ltd, 10 Alcorn Avenue, Toronto, Ontario, Canada M4V 3B2
Penguin Books (N.Z.) Ltd, 182-190 Wairau Road, Auckland 10, New Zealand

Penguin Books Ltd, Registered Offices: Harmondsworth, Middlesex, England

First published in the United States of America by HarperCollins, 1991
Published in a Puffin Easy-to-Read edition by Puffin Books,
a member of Penguin Putnam Books for Young Readers, 1999

1 3 5 7 9 10 8 6 4 2

Text copyright © Harriet Ziefert, 1991
Illustrations copyright © Mavis Smith, 1991

LIBRARY OF CONGRESS CATALOGING-IN-PUBLICATION DATA

Ziefert, Harriet.
Bob and Shirley : a tale of two lobsters / by Harriet Ziefert ; pictures by Mavis Smith.
p. cm. — (Puffin science easy-to-read)
Summary: Two large, old lobsters are caught and put in a tank in a fish store window
until some concerned humans picket the store. Based on a true story.
ISBN 0-14-038792-7
[1. Lobsters—Fiction. 2. Animal rights—Fiction.] I. Smith,
Mavis, ill. II. Title. III. Series.
PZ7.Z487Bo 1999 [E]—dc21 98-20574 CIP AC

Puffin® and Easy-to-Read® are registered trademarks of Penguin Books USA Inc.

Printed in Hong Kong

Reading Level 2.0

BOB AND SHIRLEY

A TALE OF TWO LOBSTERS

by Harriet Ziefert
pictures by Mavis Smith

PUFFIN BOOKS

Bob and Shirley were lobster friends.
Shirley was at least 40 years old.
Bob was younger than Shirley.
How much younger, no one knew.

Bob and Shirley lived a quiet life.
Their home was in the cool ocean waters
near Maine.
They crawled together
along the ocean floor.

One day, Bob and Shirley were caught
in a net.

They were taken to Rhode Island.
A worker put bands
around their big claws.

Then Bob and Shirley were sold.

They were packed in a box with ice.
They were trucked to New York.

Bob and Shirley spent the night in a crate.

The next morning, they were packed again.

They were taken to a Philadelphia fish market.

The fish store owner proudly placed Bob and Shirley in a big tank in his window.

Lots of people came to look
at the two big lobsters from Maine.

A painter saw the two lobsters.
"How much?" he asked.

The store owner answered,
"For Bob—$128. For Shirley—$160.
If you take them both, I'll make it $270."

"It's a deal!" said the painter.
"I'll be back on Friday."

At the end of the week,
many people stood
outside the fish market with signs.

The owner did not like having
angry people outside his shop.
He called the painter.
The painter agreed to buy smaller lobsters
instead of Bob and Shirley.

Bob and Shirley were packed in boxes again.

They were put on an airplane.
They were sent back to Maine.

At the airport, they were loaded onto a truck.
They were driven to the dock.

A lobsterman picked up Bob by his tail.
He lifted Bob over the side of his boat.

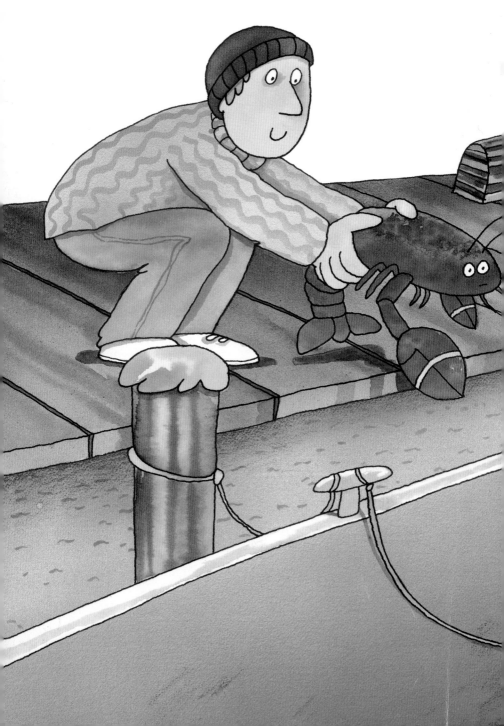

Another lobsterman lifted Shirley onto the same boat.

The lobsterman pulled away from the dock.
He headed toward the open sea.

After half an hour, he stopped.
He cut the bands from Bob's claws.
He put him back into the sea.

"He's a Maine lobster," the man said.
"This is where he belongs."

Then the lobsterman returned Shirley
to the sea.

Now Bob and Shirley were free to swim
side by side—perhaps for another 40 years.

SCIENCE FUN

1. *Bob and Shirley* is based on a true story. Tell or write a true story about an animal. If you like, draw pictures and make your own storybook.

2. Draw a picture of a lobster. Can you label these body parts?

body   claws   legs   tail
eyes   feelers (*antennae*)

3. Like lobsters, many animals are protected by laws. Some of these animals are in danger. They could become *extinct* (die out) like the dinosaurs. How many extinct animals can you name? If you don't know any, how could you find out?